Alfred. Trumble

George Inness

A memorial of the student, the artist, and the man

Alfred. Trumble

George Inness
A memorial of the student, the artist, and the man

ISBN/EAN: 9783743304321

Manufactured in Europe, USA, Canada, Australia, Japa

Cover: Foto ©Raphael Reischuk / pixelio.de

Manufactured and distributed by brebook publishing software
(www.brebook.com)

Alfred. Trumble

George Inness

Mr Joseph Lecker

Compliments of

William B Clarke.

April 25 1895.

By Courtesy of The Century Company.

GEORGE INNESS.

George Inness, N. A.

A Memorial

of

The Student, the Artist, and the Man.

By

ALFRED TRUMBLE.

———•✦•———

"THE COLLECTOR,"
454 West 24th Street,
New York City.
1895.

Printed by WILLIAM GREEN, 324 to 330 Pearl Street, New York City.

OF AN EDITION

Limited to One Hundred and Fifty,

This copy is

No. *Thirty-six*

Alf Trumble

New York City, April 23ᵈ 1895.

EXPLANATORY.

THE basis of this monograph is a study of the late George Inness, published in THE COLLECTOR, in October, 1894. The compilation of this study was caused by the death of **the** artist. Having undertaken it as a matter of duty and interest to **American** art, **the** writer had no idea of the difficulty of the task. Great an artist as George Inness was, and widely known as he was, the biographical material relating to him was meagre. The collection of the facts of his life given in the paper alluded to, and here presented with revisions and expansions, necessitated a persistent, close, and widely-distributed inquiry, which convinced the inquirer that, no other adequate record of the American Master existing, it was but just that he should be chronicled in a more worthy form, if only for the information of future and more competent chroniclers. This is **the** origin of the present monograph, and its only excuse.

ALFRED TRUMBLE.

GEORGE INNESS.

I.

A T a time when the art of this country is in a state of transition; when the methods of thought and execution of the past have given place to the radically different ones of the present; when our painters are in a tentative and experimental condition, and their productions rather the reflection of many other views than the individual expression of original ideas, uninfluenced by external conditions, the death of an artist like George Inness assumes an importance greater than that which attaches to his mere personal loss. It means not only the disappearance from active existence of a great and original man, but of a man so great, so original, so progressive and powerful in expressiveness, that he leaves a significant void in our art; one which certainly cannot be repaired at the present time, and probably not for a long time to come.

It is with no desire to unduly exalt the dead, or disparage the living, that this statement is made. An unprejudiced examination of the existing state of landscape art in America can lead to no other conclusion. Leaving aside the older school, that which has grown up in the present generation presents two strongly marked divisions. One is composed of men who have been materially influenced by the French school of 1830, and in lesser number and of more recent date by the existing school of Holland, and who, having fallen into a certain manner of thought and expression, are content to travel the single path which they have made for themselves, or have adapted themselves to; the other, of a newer contingent, whose art ideal is that created by the reactionary French school of the present, to which Manet gave the impetus, which gave origin to the title impressionism, and which Monet, the present high priest of the cult, might term, as his admirers do term it, the school of the luministes. In the former case, we have a class of artists whose merit, frequently great, is still limited by comparatively narrow boundaries; in the other, painters whose highest ambition is imitative, and who, no matter how great their dexterity and technical skill, are, in every essential sense, mere followers of men who may, in their way, style themselves pioneers.

7

Among these contemporaries George Inness towered **as a giant. He had come** into art in the time of the old school, which the moderns **so frankly despise. He,** too, had been subject to the influence of the great Frenchmen, **who so completely** revolutionized the art of their century. His earlier works exhibited the weaknesses of the art, which was popular in this country when his art life began. **Later,** one could trace the bearing which the studies involved by his earlier visits to Europe had upon his mind, and which, by broadening his views, and emancipating his hand, commenced to give his genius its destined direction. He had set forth by following a road beaten out by others. Now he struck aside, and beat a track out for himself. The spirit which had warmed his youth into studious life, now flamed up into the fire of the explorer: profound thought, the vague, half-formed ideas, which are the spurs to what we call inspiration, created in him an ambition as restless as the winds and the tides, and at the same juncture nerved him, heart and hand. Yet, with all his confidence in himself, he was always his own sternest critic : a man, always in action, always **advancing, and** never satisfied with the manner or result of his improvement, grows old only in years.

In fact, as far as his art was concerned, George Inness never revealed the weakness which is almost invariably the accompaniment of advancing years. From the time his individuality boldly declared itself, say about a quarter of a century ago, his processes continued to expand and amplify in force. This period, upon which his permanent reputation will rest, itself possesses two distinct phases. In the first, he still retained a measure of his earlier feeling and the influences which affected it. In the second, and last, he had absolutely cast off every trammel. **At an age when men** commonly settle in fixed grooves, he had no prescribed way of working. His only way was to improve upon himself, to drive on, to compel to-morrow to outdo to-day. No man, probably, had ever less vanity in himself. It was not, with him, a matter of pride in what he did, but an absorbing craving, a burning and irresistible impulse, to do what he dreamed of doing, and hoped to do in the end. How far he progressed toward the attainment of this ambition his works remain to testify. Perhaps it is not even just to call it an ambition, for with him his art was a religion, and his one desire in pursuing it the desire of a devotee. No man, certainly, could have been more indifferent to what reward of honorable esteem or substantial profit it brought him. Struggle and poverty; recognition and success, were alike to him. He lived in his art and for his art alone.

It has been truly said that to thoroughly understand the art of an artist one must not only know his works, but know the man himself. In no instance could this be truer than in that of George Inness.

II.

The life of a man naturally of the most delicate sensibilities, of a high-strung nervous temperament, of studious and self-investigatory habits, and the simplest personal tastes, is never characterized by particularly eventful episodes. When such a man, moreover, is completely bound up in the pursuit which he has selected for himself, making it part of his body and his soul, and allowing the world to move around him as it may list, his existence is passed in a realm of his own creation, to which few penetrate; and of these, fewer still really comprehend him. Without **being** actually a recluse, such a man lives a life apart. To merely know him is not to understand him. He must be studied, as well as known, if one would even approximately arrive at an appreciation of himself and his aims.

I knew, and know of, no other American artist of distinction, except William Page, who in any way resembled George Inness in his mental characteristics. Curiously enough, both were born in almost the same section, Page at Albany, N. Y., in 1811, and Inness about two miles west of Newburg, in 1825. Thus Page was fourteen years the senior of his contemporary, and as he died in 1885, their limit of life was about the same. Page, like Inness, was devoted to the study of metaphysics, and to weaving the theories and ideas he derived from them with his art. They studied in the same mystic-theological field, and to a certain point there was a most interesting resemblance in their theorizations. But Page suffered the calamity of a failure of his mental powers, which rendered the last decade of his life practically a blank. Moreover, far as he advanced in art—and in relation to his time he advanced very far—he never completely released himself from the influence of the Italian school of the past, and particularly of Titian, of whom he had made a special study, whereas Inness not only asserted himself distinctly many years before he ceased to labor, but never halted by the way, and retained his intellectual powers to the last. Page, too, was a man singularly deficient in the command of language, either as a conversationalist or a writer, while Inness was especially fluent and eloquent both with speech and pen. In their art the two men resembled each other, to an extent, in their love and command of color, but the color of Page was a splendid convention **only, based** on the study of pictures, while that of Inness was instinct with the ever-vital splendor of nature herself.

The date of George Inness's birth is given as May 1, 1825. Delicate from childhood, and gifted with the most exquisite nervous sensitiveness, the boy must have seemed predestined to a life of vicissitudes and trouble. He was a reader from the time he learned to read, and a creature of his own imagination from the time his mind received the impressions of his reading. He often told how, in his childhood, awful and even frightful dreams would rouse him from his sleep, and send him scouring about the darkness of the house, until his nerves composed themselves sufficiently to permit him to seek repose again.

Such a special incident is trifling in itself. It was but the result of extreme mental tension on a timorous child. But when it is borne in view in tracing the course of the artist through his life and his working career, it is a clear indication of his character of mind, and an index to those later leanings of thought which exercised such powerful influence on his art.

Young Inness's parents settled in Newark, N. J., while he was a boy. In the latter city, at the age of about fourteen years, he received some, apparently not very

9

regular, lessons in drawing from an old drawing-master named Barker. The condition of his health probably did not permit of his assiduous application to his instructions, but he himself considered that he had secured a fair groundwork for the future from his pedagogue of the pencil. His one ambition, while under his tutelage, was to some day learn to draw as well as his master, and, as he once naïvely remarked to me, "I think the best thing that can happen to a boy is to have some honest ambition stirred up in him, no matter how trifling it may be." That the ambition was not trifling in this case, circumstances abundantly proved.

The elder Inness desired to train his son for a commercial career, but in this the youth proved entirely intractable. A month's service in a store, which his father set up for him, according to his own admission, resulted in his losing all his customers. Meantime his passion for drawing suggested another practical vocation for him. Like his great French contemporary, Charles Jacque, he was set to work as a map engraver, with the firm of Sherman & Smith, in New York City. He did not endure this drudgery even as long as did Jacque, for he abandoned it at the end of a year, almost broken in health from the confinement to which it subjected him. Becoming partially restored, he returned to his copper plates, but soon left them again for good. The experience had, however, done him that much service that it had assisted in the training of his eye and hand, and a brief course of sketching from nature which he now undertook, with his Newark home for headquarters, showed a considerable advancement in his powers. His color sense had now been aroused, and the desire to be a painter had grown into a determination. He was now a young man of twenty years, capable of judging for himself, and precarious as the career of an artist then was in America, his wishes were no longer opposed.

There was at that time in New York a French artist of some popularity, Regis Gignoux. He was but nine years the senior of young Inness, but had enjoyed the advantage of study in France, both in the provinces and in Paris, where he was a pupil of Paul Delaroche. Gignoux had been two years in this country, painting American landscapes, which secured esteem in their day, when Inness came to him as a pupil, and from him received, during a few months, the only direct instruction as a painter that he ever obtained. It served him in so far that it gave him sufficient insight in the handling of color to prosecute his independent investigations of that great problem, and he set himself to work to master it, in a studio of his own, in 1846.

His beginnings were naturally humble. To receive $25 for a picture was a triumph for him. But the pictures themselves did not satisfy him. He knew that he was groping in the dark. He was painting as others around him were painting, but he was not painting as he felt, and as he wished to paint. These things, he argued with himself, were not nature. They had none of the spirit of nature in them. They were mere colored drawings, inspired with none of the movement and vitality that he felt instinctively, when he looked abroad at forest and farmland, and mountain, river and sky.

"One afternoon," he said, "when I was completely dispirited and disgusted, I gave over work and went out for a walk. In a print-shop window I noticed an engraving after one of the old masters. I do not remember what picture it was. I could not then analyze that which attracted me in it, but it fascinated me. The print seller showed me others, and they repeated the same sensation in me. There was a power of motive, a bigness of grasp in them. They were nature, rendered grand instead of being belittled by trifling detail and puny execution. I commenced to take them out to nature with me, to compare them with her as she really appeared, and the light began to dawn. I had no originals to study, but I found some of their qualities in paintings by Cole and Durand to which I had access. There was a lofty striving in Cole, although he did not technically realize that for which he reached. There was in Durand a more intimate feeling of nature. 'If,' thought I, 'these two can only be combined! I will try!'"

The spirit then aroused in the youth of twenty was still active in the man of three score and ten, when his brush was finally stricken from his hand.

III.

Experimenting and working on the lines which he thus laid down for himself, Inness's ability began to make an impression and his pictures to attract attention. The American Art Union, which was then in successful operation, purchased from him. He found some individual patrons—among them the dry goods auctioneer, Ogden Haggerty, who not only bought his pictures, but proposed to him to defray his expenses for a trip to Europe. Early in 1847 he sailed for England, whence he soon passed over to Italy, where he remained more than a year, painting principally in Rome or the vicinity. He here commenced to really form what might be called a style—a style in which one can distinguish the influence of the classic art of the landscape masters of the past, but which still has the impress of a certain individuality. The effect which this Italian sojourn had upon him was much akin to that which the Englishman, Richard Wilson, had experienced a century before.

He returned to New York, but, restless in spirit, spurred by a keen sense of deficiency, and conscious that he had not carried his studies far enough, he, in 1850, took flight across the Atlantic again, this time to France. French art at that time was in the full swing of a triumphant revolution. The league of giants—Millet, Corot, Delacroix, Rousseau, Dupré, Decamps, Jacque, Diaz—were battering down the last ruins of the walls of conventionalism with colossal blows. The air was full of the contagion of battle against the artificial and the false in art. Amid this enthusiastic awakening, the impressionable American would not have been himself had he not become infected by it. He lived, as he said, in a sort of stupor of intellectual amazement, working almost mechanically, but instinctively in the direction which he felt to be the true one.

His return to America, after a sojourn of a year abroad, found him the first of our landscape painters to essay the application and expression of the developments which were then riding on their high tide in France. His works of this period, in many instances, show this influence very clearly, but his art remained uneven and indicative of the conflict he was waging with himself. In some of his pictures he displays his old elaboration of detail, in others he works broadly, simply and directly to the point. If he had been a merely imitative man, he would have fallen into either the Italian or the French style, and been lost. **But to him life was but another** name for progress, and the lessons conveyed by the works of others only a stimulus to the solution of the newer problems they inspired.

He spent four years in New England, amid the lovely rural scenery of which Medfield, Mass., is the centre. Thence, after another European visit, he removed in order to make a settlement at Eaglewood, in a picturesque country near Perth Amboy, N. J. Up to this time he had not formulated the ideas to which he endeavored to give artistic expression. They remained vague and conflicting, and reflected themselves in the divergences and inequalities of his works.

During his first sojourn in Italy, William Page was settled in Rome. Page, who from his youth had been inclined to mysticism, and who had such strong religious tendencies that he had even contemplated adopting the ministry, had taken up the study of **the theology of Emanuel** Swedenborg, to which he became a convert. Whether this had drawn Inness's attention in the same direction, or whether he took up the theme independently, I do not know. Indeed, I have often imagined that he did not know himself. It is possible that Page may have influenced him, especially as the latter had his home at Tottenville, Staten Island, just across the ferry from Perth Amboy. At any rate, during the half dozen years of his residence at Eaglewood, George Inness's entire leisure from his easel was occupied in the investigation of the Swedenborgian principles involved in the doctrine of **divine humanity, and it** was out of this doctrine that he drew that which may, **with perfect propriety, be** called the religion of his art.

In view of the important, and indeed ultimately supreme, influence this adoption of faith exercised on his art, it is just as well to clearly and briefly review it here. The grand and distinctive principle of the Swedenborgian theology, next to the doctrine of the divine humanity, is the doctrine of life. According to this latter, God alone lives. All creation, man included, is dead. Our apparent life, the life of the earth itself, is but the divine presence, which exists in individuals and in objects in different degrees; in trees, plants, stones, the waters, air and sky. It was the later belief of George Inness, that he worked ever under the instruction and guidance of a divine power, which gave direction to his labor and guided him to a comprehension of the significance of what he painted, and to the truthful expression of it. In a conversation with Mr. George W. Sheldon,* one of his biographers, he once said:

"The whole effort and aim of the true artist is to eschew whatever is individual, whatever is the result of the influence of his own evil nature, of his own carnal lusts, and to acknowledge nothing but the inspiration that comes from truth and goodness, or the divine principle within him, nothing but the one personality, or God, who is the centre of man, and the source of all noble inspiration." Man, his argument

---

* See appendix.

12

proceeds, is no more a mere personality than nature is mere dumb substance. Everything is animated by the spirit of God, and nothing can be represented truthfully unless this spirit is recognized with love and reverence. "I would not give a fig," he goes on, "for art ideas except as they represent what I perceive behind them; and I love to think most of what I, in common with all men, need most—the good of our practice in the art of life. Rivers, streams, the rippling brook, the hillside, the sky, clouds—all things we see—will convey the sentiment of the highest art if we are in the love of God and the desire of truth."

This was, in substance, the theology which George Inness worked out during his residence at Eaglewood, and which later, year by year, he worked more closely into his art. When he was not endeavoring to paint it he was writing it, not with any special idea of giving it to the public, but for the purpose of more closely examining and expounding it for himself. After a long day's labor in his studio, he would refresh himself with a long night at his desk. After a day of disappointment at his easel, through failure to secure upon the canvas that subtle spirituality which he saw, or rather felt, in his subject as its soul, he would turn for fresh enlightenment and inspiration to his manuscripts, and seek in them the clue which he had lost.

IV.

George Inness was made an associate of the National Academy of Design in 1853, and in 1868, during his residence at Eaglewood, was elected a full member. After leaving his New Jersey home, and spending about a year in New York, he in 1871 made another voyage to Europe, this time remaining four years in Rome and Paris. The pictures which he produced during this period are much broader and simpler in treatment than many which preceded them, and more studied in style. Oddly enough, although he had for some years been working upon his Swedenborgian studies, he did not, to any notable extent, begin to apply his conclusions yet. He may still have been meditating upon them without having brought them into practical form, or he may have been influenced by his surroundings. The peculiar character of the Italian scenes in which he found himself, their romantic historical associations and classical atmosphere, were likely to produce an impression on his mind which would repeat itself in his work. Even when at his best in his European subjects, he was never really himself, as he was when he treated our native scenery; never upon other motives did his personality stamp itself so strongly.

He spent the first year after his return in Boston, where his art had long before found admirers, and then returned to New York, where he maintained a studio until he removed to his home at Montclair, N. J. His worldly condition at this time was by no means commensurate with his merits, though he had left his years of actual, serious struggle, behind him. A limited number of appreciative collectors found pleasure in his works, and his sales at the exhibitions were moderately good. But none of the commercial circumstances of life affected him in the slightest degree. He continued to paint, to develop his metaphysical theories, and was content, if not

happy. His industry was extraordinary, but, in spite of his incessant diligence, the amount of his productiveness was limited by the system under which he produced.

During this period in New York he at various times occupied a studio adjoining that of his son-in-law, Mr. Jonathan Scott Hartley, the sculptor, in one of the studio buildings in West Fifty-fifth street, and others in the University Building and at Booth's Theatre. It was his custom to paint standing, and while his method of execution was rapid at the starting of a picture, his speed would diminish as he advanced, and as the difficulty of realizing the result he aimed at grew upon him, canvas after canvas would be set aside and another subject commenced. There were invariably from a dozen to a score of these pictures, in various stages of progress, in the studio. Occasionally, in a happy mood, he would complete one. Often he would cover one with an entirely different subject. Frequently a picture far advanced, and perhaps even completed, would arouse his dissatisfaction, and he would fall to and alter it completely, not rarely for the worse. His peculiar energy and nervous excitement at his work, on such occasions, had about it the suggestion of a battle. And, indeed, it was a battle the artist was fighting, with the impulse of genius to nerve his hand.

His day began early and ended late. If it happened to find him in a favorable spirit, his industry continued unflaggingly, hour by hour. Even the incursion of a visitor would not interrupt it. He would pursue his work as he talked, perhaps dilating upon the theory of which his brush provided practical illustration. If an idle mood came on him, the palette and brushes were laid aside, a cigar-box probably produced, and he would fill the interval of relaxation with a veritable dissertation upon his favorite subject. Even when he did not happen to have a listener, he found relief in uttering his thoughts aloud. On his bad days, when he could not paint, when whatever he set his brush to went wrong in his eyes, he would stride the room, carrying on one of these discourses with himself, or go to visit other artists until the spirit rose in him again, and he resumed his task. Either in speech or in his art, his incessant mental activity had to be provided with some vent.

It was, perhaps, under these circumstances that the personality of this extraordinary man could be best studied. Where weaker men demand retirement for the performance of their work, he lived in it so completely, and thought and action were so thoroughly interwoven with him, that one then came closest to George Inness as he was. At periods of absolute idleness, when he was physically worn out, for example, or when the necessity of travel or some other cause separated him from the labor which was his joy, he to a great extent relapsed into himself, and, while always of a genial and pleasant manner, did not reveal himself in any approximate degree. There were, in effect, two George Innesses. The perfect one was he in whom the sorcery of his work charmed into life all the latent and dormant forces of the great mind of which that work was the result, and in its fashion remains the index.

He was a man of the middle stature, of a spare frame, with a face full of character, and gray, penetrating eyes. He wore the thin beard of a man whose face had never known the touch of the razor, and his broad brow was framed in a mass of long and always disorderly hair. A bust of him by his son-in-law, Mr. Hartley, while somewhat idealized, gives still an excellent general idea of his features. He was always careless in his dress, so that the picturesque *ensemble* of head and figure was not disturbed. His movements were rapid with nervous energy, and when he became interested in conversation or discussion, his gestures were instinctively appropriate, and, like the action of his body, full of spirit. I do not remember any orator or player who ever conveyed more force in his physical accompaniment of his words, or more harmoniously joined the action to the word. Indeed, if he had chosen to expound his views upon the rostrum, his command of language, his bursts of nobly-phrased enthusiasm, and his frequent, fluent flights of a lofty eloquence would, I am sure, have held even a skeptical audience under a spell.

He, however, while never affecting the habit of a recluse, avoided, as far as possible, all public prominence. He took no active part in the movements of the artistic societies to which he belonged, beyond contributing to their exhibitions. He held the feuds and cabals of the contending factions of art in the greatest aversion, and viewed the sensational devices adopted on occasions to give the art he worshipped the vulgar popular attractiveness of a circus, with indignant scorn. For medals or other awards of honor or merit, at the hands of committees or juries, he cherished an outspoken contempt. He believed in the artist as an artist, and in his art as its own best reward. "Think, work, do your best," he said. "If the world does not then appreciate you, what satisfaction can a diploma or a medal bring? They are only the recognition of a few men, who appreciate you anyhow, and they go to so many who are not worthy of them, that they do not carry any real significance to those who may deserve them. Pass your verdict upon yourself, if you are capable of criticising yourself. The verdict of the world will be passed in due time, and it will be a just one, even if it does not sustain that of prize committees and juries of award."

There are painters among us who claim the distinction of having been pupils of George Inness, but I know of no such claim which is not based upon a very frail foundation. The door of Inness's studio was never closed against a young man of any ability. His advice and suggestion were as free as the songs of the wild birds. From his own struggling past, of which the memory never was lost to him, he knew the value of that encouragement and counsel which had been denied to him, and which, as part of the duty of his life, he never denied to others. But a teacher he never was. I question if even his son, an artist of great merit, who has inherited much of his father's ability as well as his name, was ever a pupil of his in the strict sense. I remember, one bleak winter evening, when the snow was deep and crusted with rime, encountering Inness as he was plodding homeward from his studio, and we went on together. I was just from the studio of a painter who, in speaking of his own life to me, had somewhat boastfully claimed to have been the "favorite pupil" of George Inness, so I asked the master whether he had had many pupils in his time.

"I have had one for a very long time," he replied, smiling in his peculiar way, "and he is more than enough for me. The more I teach him the less he knows, and the older he grows the farther he is from what he ought to be."

It was not necessary to inquire the name of this intractable neophyte, of course.

15

V.

When George Inness came from Boston to make his final settlement in New York, a movement of great significance to the art of America was already making itself felt. The revolt—for such, in fact, it was—of the younger painters against the National Academy was in ferment. The older and the newer elements in the artistic body were distinctly, and even in many cases violently, antagonistic. The former saw a threat in the invasion of a little army of talented and energetic men, fresh with the spirit of youth and strong in the best training of the great schools of Europe. As for the latter, they made no hesitation in expressing their contempt for the antiquated methods of their elders, feeble at least where they were not absolutely false; and what respect could they entertain personally for an artistic body leading members of which boldly avowed in print such sentiments as:

"Corot is incomplete and slovenly. His landscapes are ghosts of landscapes. They have neither technical nor literary excellence."

"I am not an admirer of Millet. His pictures are coarse and vulgar in character; they are repulsive. . . . Troyon's paintings are rather coarse in character. I shouldn't call him a colorist by any means."

"I can't think anything of Corot. I can't understand him."

"Delacroix is a mere botch. He could not draw, he had no idea of composition, he flung his color at you like a brickbat; he is as horrible as Millet, who strikes you as one of his brutal peasants might hit you with a club."

Is it any wonder that the newcomers, in spite of the excellent reception given to their works by the Academy, in the memorable exhibition of 1876, should have failed to see in the professors of such principles any promise of sympathy, or that they should resolve to form a society of their own for mutual encouragement and defense? The marvel would have been that they had not done so.

Most of the stronger members of the Academy, it is true, even when they were not in sympathy with the new movement, were opposed to treating it inhospitably; but the Academy had become, in a manner, compacted on trade union principles, and **upon** the strong men had fallen the unwritten but accepted obligation of carrying the weaklings. So the Society of American Artists came into existence, and an undercurrent of ill-feeling set in between the two institutions, which even now, with all the liberal concessions made by the Academy, still runs a sluggish course, although it has, happily, nearly run itself out.

In this feud George Inness, although an Academician, had no part. Both parties recognized the distinction of his art, and he was one of the first of a group of his *confrères* of the Academy to be elected into the new brotherhood. But he had already got beyond the necessity, as he had certainly always been beyond any active desire, for such recognition. The tide had turned, and was setting in his favor with ever-growing volume. Where formerly collectors had purchased a picture or two by him, they now commenced to collect them. About 1875 Mr. Thomas B. Clarke began the acquisitions which have resulted in a group of Innesses, in his private collection,

which number some twenty-five examples of the first quality. The late George I.
Seney was, I believe, his next liberal patron. Others followed, who will be alluded
to elsewhere. A collective exhibition of his works, at the American Art Galleries, in
1885, gave additional impetus to his fortunes, and as far as the material problem of an
artist's life is concerned, his victory was won.

But in his art he remained in the lists. His was not a nature to be satisfied with
standing still. He had built himself a studio adjoining the old Dodge mansion, which
he had purchased, in a beautiful situation near Montclair, N. J. There, and during
his excursions to New England, Nova Scotia, Virginia, California, he continued his
grapple for his ideal, and the fruit was the series of pictures in his now pronounced
and most broadly simplified style, which he continued until almost the day of his
departure on the journey which was destined to be his last. He had, perhaps, never
been happier during his long career than he was at his Montclair retreat. He was
superior to all commercial necessities, and independent of relations which might
have imposed any trammels upon his art. He could paint what he chose, and as he
chose. He was surrounded by scenes congenial in character, and located in a spot
favorable for the observation of those moods of nature which he strove to interpret,
as expressions of her soul and his own. His occasional journeys provided him with
a variety to his subjects of study, and sent him back with his eye and mind refreshed
for the discovery of new beauties in the familiar scenes. It is not unnatural that
some of his brethren in art, perhaps not without a pang of envy, looked upon this
later period of his life as an artist's ideal of existence.

He had sailed his bark through troubled waters, ruffled by many storms, to a safe
and restful haven. He lived like a patriarch, with his son and daughter and their
families for neighbors. He was secure in the world's esteem and honor, and in the
love and respect of faithful friends. He had won, by fifty years of devotion to **his art**
and fidelity to his conscience, his place at the head of the art of the century. The
most ambitious of men would desire no more; yet, his only ambition, as he watched
from his cottage door the dawn and sunset, the burning noonday and the serene
splendor of the moonlight, the summer storm rolling down the hillsides, and the
winter tempest driving in shrill blasts over wastes of snow, was to penetrate the
great secret they embodied, and to fathom in them the mysterious heart that stirs the
universe.

VI.

The representative work of George Inness—that is to say, the work in which he
figures with his most intense and distinctive individuality—is that which exhibits itself in native subjects. The range of these is very wide. It extends practically from
Canada to Mexico and from the Atlantic to the Pacific. New Jersey, New York and
New England, which, in the order noted, formed his first fields of study, seem always
to have remained his favorites. That a subject was ever with him a matter of
deliberate selection is doubtful. His choice depended upon impulse. He painted in

17

sight of Mount Washington for days, until, upon one special day, some unusual effect of hour or weather on the mountain itself impressed him, and he painted it. He saw Niagara a dozen or a score of times, before it had grown into him as **the subject** of a picture. Even when he went so far as to make a sketch or study of a spot, **this** memorandum might lie by for years **before he took it up to work upon, or it might** never be touched again.

In a man of less profound thought, of less persistent self-examination, of less rigorous exploration of the causes from which effects spring, this indecision might have been laid to mere whim. With him it proceeded from the absolute necessity he was under of experiencing an emotion. He was past-master of all the technical resources of his art. He had carried his experiments in the possibilities of the palette **to an** almost incredible length. He could draw with accuracy and strength. Yet he could not, by any exercise of will, have compelled himself to paint what he did not feel—to produce mechanically what took no grasp upon his heart. A poet may some-times be obscure, may fail in attaining to his highest pitch of eloquence, but he can-not write doggerel, not from inability to jingle words together, but from inability to force himself to the odious task. In a similar sense George Inness could not paint doggerel. He might not always succeed in a picture. He sometimes, even often-times, did not. But it is certain that in every picture which he gave out in his later years he believed that he had mastered its spirit, or had as nearly mastered it as lay within his power.

When he was mistaken in this, it was simply because he had unconsciously mis-calculated **the depth and** receptiveness of his own emotions, or, according to his own doctrine, because he had failed to purify himself to the **standard** of his subject, and therefore was neither capable of reaching its vital spirit nor of defining the extent to which he had fallen short. The greatest of artists cannot avoid producing some in-different works, for the greater the artist the more difficult are the tasks which he sets himself to perform. Infallibility is the gift of no mortal being.

But what a panorama of nature does this man spread before you: Landscapes of **autumn,** splendid in their imperial vestments of purple, crimson and gold; the slumber-**ous** silence of midsummer, brooding over drowsing fields and forests, in which the **very leaves** have sunk to sleep; spreading meadowlands, with their verdure bejew-**eled with the dew of** morning; nature by day and night, and at every period of the **day or night; under every** joyous, sad or tragic aspect, at all seasons, in all weathers, in fertile **valleys, in towering crags,** splintered by the tempests of ages; on ironbound coasts, **whose cliffs tremble at** the savage onsets of the stormy sea. Could **mere** painting convey such an impression to you? Could mere painting bring to your nostrils this perfume of the rich sod, wet with the softly descending rain; bring to your ears the piping of the robin, which salutes the dawn from its nest in the road-side brambles; bring to your senses the languor of this Indian summer day, in its bridal-veil of soft haze? Could mere mechanical artifice send the thunder rolling down those hillsides, deafen you with the crashing fall of yonder cataract, or charm you with the chime of that spring rivulet, released from its winter bondage and dancing merrily over its pebbly bed? What work of hand and eye, soever cunning, could produce this sorcery without the direction of a master sentiment of magnetic power?

"The true purpose of the painter," according to Inness, "is simply to reproduce in other minds the impression which a scene has made upon **him. A** work of art does not appeal to the intellect. It does not appeal to the moral sense. Its aim is not to instruct, not to edify, but to awaken an emotion. This emotion may be one of love, of pity, of veneration, of hate, of pleasure, or of pain; but it must be a single emotion, if the work has unity, as every such work should have, and the true beauty of the work consists in the beauty of the sentiment or emotion which it inspires. Its real greatness consists in the quality and the force of this emotion. Details in the picture must be elaborated only enough fully to reproduce the impression which the artist wishes to reproduce. When more than this is done, the impression is weakened or lost, and we see simply an array of external things, which may be very cleverly painted and may look very real, but which do not make an artistic painting. The effort and the difficulty of an artist are to combine the two, namely, to make the thought clear and preserve the unity of impression."

Upon another point he held. "There is a notion that objective force is inconsistent with poetic representation. But this is a very grave error. What is often called poetry is a mere jingle of rhyme—intellectual dishwater. The poetic quality is not obtained by eschewing any truths of fact or of nature which can be included in a harmony or real representation. Poetry is the vision of reality."

In these two utterances one may discern a perfectly simple and lucid exposition of the formula by which, for fifteen or twenty years, George Inness had been gradually working forward toward the results embodied in his latest works. Reduced to a single paragraph it is: "Put just enough in a picture to **present the main theme** without distracting attention from this centre of interest, and **take no wanton liber-**ties with the subject in order to produce an artificial effect at the expense of truth."

VII.

The most original genius whom the art of England ever produced was J. W. M. Turner. This strange and inspired man, born in a squalid barber-shop in a dirty London court, deprived of every advantage of education by the poverty of his father, tainted, perhaps, by the madness of his poor, demented mother, rose resplendent from the mire which bred him, as the beautiful old fable tells us that the phœnix soars, revivified, from the ashes of its own destruction, by that same force which the phœnix typifies. The fable of the phœnix has been variously expounded by various dealers in idle phrases, but if it be analyzed from the standpoint of common sense, its meaning, it seems to me, must be plain. It is the type of human energy and resolution, inspired by the confidence which comes of innate power, which defies disaster and mocks misfortune by its indomitable faith in its own potentialities. The man who has something in him will work it out, no matter what obstacles he may find opposed to him.

An old gentleman whom I knew in London, had known Turner very well. He had formed a very remarkable collection of his pictures and sketches, and had purchased most of them personally from the artist. He was one of the last men who had visited Turner's house before he wandered off to Chelsea, to die in a garret overlooking the Thames, which he loved to watch making its shining pathway to the sea. This gentleman told me that on one occasion, while Turner was signing for him a set of proofs of the "Liber Studiorum," which he had purchased, he made some remark which brought this work into comparison with the "Liber Veritatis" of Claude Lorraine.

"That," said Turner, in his rude, brutal way, "is no praise for me and no honor **to Claude.** D—n the proofs! I'll sign no more to-day." Nor would he.

In the same way, the comparisons which have been instituted, at certain sources, between George Inness and Corot and Rousseau, are both unjust and absurd. As I have shown, Inness undoubtedly was impressed by the movement in the van of which the two great Frenchmen figured, but the profit he derived from their example was that of suggestion solely. His style was as distinct from theirs as their styles were from each other. He appreciated and esteemed them, as his frequent criticisms showed. In a comparison of Meissonier and Corot he remarked: "If a painter could unite Meissonier's careful reproduction of details with Corot's inspirational power, he would be the very god of art. But Corot's art is higher than Meissonier's. Let Corot paint a rainbow, and his work reminds you of the poet's description, 'The rainbow is the spirit of flowers.' Let Meissonier paint a rainbow, and his work reminds you of a definition in chemistry. The one is poetic truth, the other is scientific truth; the former is æsthetic, the latter analytic." Of Millet he said: "Millet is one of those artistic angels whose aim was to represent pure and holy human sentiments—sentiments which speak of home, of love, of labor, of sorrow, and so on. Many of his pictures, indeed, display weaknesses to which minds like his are at times particularly liable, as though the strength of flesh and blood had overcome the power of the spirit. But he is the very first in that class of painters who reproduce such sentiments in their paintings, and in his paintings do we find the highest of these sentiments."

"Rousseau," he said, "was perhaps the greatest French landscape painter," but it was with Corot and Daubigny that he always expressed the closest sympathy. They came closer to the soul of nature, while Rousseau's art was clouded by the morbid turn of his mind, which ultimately resulted in the overthrow of his reason. To Decamps and Delacroix he gave a high rating. Turner he considered not a genius of the first order, not as great and genuine an artist as Constable, but "a great scene painter." In all his criticism Inness was straightforward and outspoken with the voice of personal conviction. The last printed utterances of his were made some twelve months before, and in part reported verbatim in a New York newspaper after his death. This passage will serve to afford a good idea of his simple and direct expression of his opinions on the current conditions of and movements in art:

"Mind you," he continued, "there is an immense deal of fine art in these French

20

exhibitions, but there is also very much that is preposterous. To obtain recognition, however, it must be French. Of the many pictures the French send over here I have seen nothing very good. Of Cazin, whom the Americans are now fussing about. I have seen nothing remarkable, though some pretty pictures."

"But you are not opposed to exhibitions, Mr. Inness?"

"Yes, I am; to competitions in art and the awarding of medals and all that sort of thing. These exhibitions are not made with sufficient care. They are too much of a jumble, so that the pictures exhibited continually conflict with one another. When it comes to the awards, they are well enough in a school where the master has certain methods and ideas of his own, because he can judge which pupils come nearest to those methods and ideas. But the artist comes out as an individual. Who is going to judge of his work when it is acknowledged that some who have proved the greatest have not been recognized at all during their lifetimes? No, the awarding of a medal to a work of art is reducing art to a sphere of mechanics. Every artist has his own feeling, and, if he develops it, may be a great master in his way, yet the other schools, the men with other methods and ideas, will not recognize the merit of his work."

"But can this matter of feeling be explained in words?"

"I think so. I have made a thorough and complete theory of it. I am seventy years of age, and the whole study of my life has been to find out what it is that is in myself—what is this thing we call life, and how does it operate. Upon these questions my ideas have become clearer and clearer, and what I hold is that the Creator never makes any two things alike, or any two men alike. Every man has a different impression of what he sees, and that impression constitutes feeling, and every man has a different feeling.

"Now, there has sprung up a new school, a mere passing fad, called impressionism, the followers of which pretend to study from nature and paint it as it is. All these sorts of things I am down on. I will have nothing to do with them. They are shams."

VIII.

George Inness was the fifth in descent of thirteen children by one mother. Of these, six are yet living. On the father's side he came of Scotch stock. The father was an energetic and thrifty man, with fairly liberal ideas. The mother was a strict housewife, and a rigid member of the Methodist persuasion, who brought her children up in the closest conformance to that creed. From earliest childhood the artist and the thinker of the future was bound down to the narrowest and severest limits of moral and religious duty.

While yet a babe in arms his father sold the Newburg farm and transported his family in a sloop—for it was before the days of Hudson River steamboats—to New York City, where he resumed the business from which he had retired on account of ill-health, prosecuting it for some four or five years. His health again failing, he abandoned it once more, and carried his family over to New Jersey. He purchased property at a location which is now almost the centre of a great manufacturing city, but which was then on the threshold of a beautiful and picturesque country. The roomy old house stood upon elevated ground, in twenty-five acres of farm land, and commanded a far-reaching view of the vast salt meadows, alive with wild fowl, and of the farms and hills on the other hand. Newark at that time was a rather bustling country town, connected with Jersey City and New York by stage lines which made two daily trips to and fro. It was not even on the regular line of travel between the then two great cities of the United States, New York and Philadelphia.

The exact location of the Inness home in Newark was on High and Nesbitt streets, now Central avenue. In 1837 the farm portion of this property was cut up into streets and lots, but the family still resided in the mansion until about 1843, when the father again removed them to New York. It was during this interval that George received such education as the schools and Academy of Newark afforded. When he was in the thirteenth or fourteenth year of his age, the principal of the Academy informed his father that it was useless to keep him at school any longer, as he spent his time mostly in drawing pictorial figures on his slate, instead of using it for mathematical purposes. Accordingly he was taken away, and his father placed him in his store, in one of his buildings in Washington street, Newark, which he had opened for this purpose, intending to bring him up in the grocery line. But his artistic mind, which was then developing, could not adapt itself to the petty details of such a business, and his carelessness and indifference made it manifest that in an employment of this character he was a failure. Therefore this project was soon abandoned, and he was placed with the drawing-master, Barker, to receive lessons in drawing and elementary painting. Some of his efforts in this latter branch are still in existence.

It was not very long before Mr. Barker notified his father that George had received from him all the education in his line he could impart, and he was then sent to New York to learn engraving. Now followed his experience as has been previously detailed, ending in his study under Gignoux, eked out with a few instructions from Asher B. Durand.

His elder brother, James A. Inness, who is now a resident of this city, was at that time living at Pottsville, Pa., and there George visited him, and painted some of his earliest pictures. His New York residence had been at the Astor House, where he had paid his board in pictures. He did much sketching in Schuylkill County, and there is record of a campaign banner which he painted for the Henry Clay Club, of Pottsville, during this visit, and which came to grief from being rolled up before the color was dry. After his return to New York, he did what most artists are prone to do when they can scarcely earn a living for themselves—he married. Misfortune attended this union from the start. The bride contracted a cold upon her wedding day, which developed into a consumption, of which she died six months later. Before he made his first visit to Europe he married again, the lady being the widow who survives him.

All of these early years were years of bitter struggle with him, and his family had more than once to come to his assistance. The production of pot-boilers was a recourse to which he was frequently compelled. Some of these are still in existence, feeble copies in color of engravings of the day, in which, however, a certain skill of hand already revealed itself. At one time three of his elder brothers kept him afloat for a year by buying whatever he painted, and disposing of the pictures where and how they could. Neither then, nor ever in his after life, had he the remotest idea of the value of money, and to relieve him of one distress was simply to provide him with an opportunity to fall into another. His contempt for the mercantile element **of life** was profound and outspoken. One of his earliest theories was that trade was under the obligation to sustain art, and that merchants were only created to support artists.

One of his elder brothers, Mr. James A. Inness, in furnishing some details of his life, says:

"I have alluded to my brother's metaphysical labors. These were taken up more as a relaxation after excessive efforts in the field of his art, than as a regular pursuit. However, he was at all times fond of discussion on social and theological problems, and at one time told me that in his early days, if his health had permitted, he would have become absorbed in metaphysical studies. His environment during his childhood and youth was extremely well calculated to give such a tendency to his active temperament and brain. His mother, who died in his **fifteenth** year, was a Methodist, and brought up her children in strict compliance with the discipline and requirements of the Methodism of that day. His aunt, who afterward became his step-mother, was as strict a Baptist, and an earnest Controversialist, whilst their brother, his uncle, was as firm a Universalist and as uncompromising in his belief. So religious topics became almost a daily subject of conversation, dispute, and a mind of George's character would naturally commence early in life an investigation of the points in dispute, and to search the scriptures for the truths thereof, probably laying **thereby** the foundation of the Swedenborgian faith, to which he became attached in later years."

Of George Inness's children, one, a daughter, died while the family resided in Rome, and is buried there in the Protestant cemetery. His son, George Inness, is a painter of great ability. His daughter is the wife of the sculptor, Jonathan Scott Hartley, N. A.

IX.

It would, of course, be impossible to trace, even with approximate accuracy, the collections or individual owners of pictures by George Inness. Previous to his later period he produced most prolifically, and his works were scattered far and wide. He told how he found and bought one of his earlier paintings in the City of Mexico; and he landed upon others in the most unexpected places—in California, Florida, Virginia, and the Pennsylvania mountains. To a man who lives by his art, his productions, until his reputation is established, are foundlings; they pass from his hands to private buyers, to dealers, into auctions, and he soon loses all trace of them. It is only when his fame has come to him that a record is kept, and even then it is far from perfect. During the last dozen years of his life Inness, while even more industrious than in his youth, issued fewer evidences of his industry to the world, because he effaced and repainted so much, and left so many works in a state which he considered incomplete. The two hundred and forty canvases sold by his executors, and which represented the collection he left in his studio, were probably but a small part of the numbers which he discarded and destroyed.

The largest single collection of Inness pictures is undoubtedly that of Mr. Thomas B. Clarke, of New York, to which I have already alluded. It is composed of works of the highest choice. The collection formed by **the late** Mr. George I. Seney was partially broken up previous to that gentleman's death, and the remainder dispersed at the sales rendered necessary by the settlement of his estate. The fine collection of Mr. Richard H. Halstead * was sold a month before the disposition of the studio collection by the Inness executors. There is a strong group of the artist's **works** in the Potter Palmer collection, in Chicago, and he is represented **there** in the collections of Mr. James W. Ellsworth, Mr. S. N. Nickerson and Mr. Martin A. Ryerson, among others. Still other appreciators and supporters of his art are to be found in Mr. T. B. Walker and Mr. T. P. Wilson, of Minneapolis, Minn.; Mr. W. K. Thaw, of Pittsburgh, Pa.; Mr. L. Z. Leiter, of Washington, D. C.; Mr. Lewis H. Blair, of Richmond, Va.; Mr. R. B. Angus and Sir William Van Horne, of Montreal, Canada, and Mr. F. J. Hecker, of Detroit, Mich. The galleries of the New York and Brooklyn collectors are naturally rich in examples of Inness, notably those of Mr. William T. Evans, Mr. George A. Hearn, Mr. Benjamin Altman, Mr. Frederic Bonner, Mr. Washington Wilson, Mr. T. J. Briggs, Mr. W. H. Fuller, Mr. Nelson Robinson, Mr. Henry Sampson, Mr. Edson Bradley, Mr. Samuel Untermeyer, Mr. E. J. Chaffee, Mr. H. R. McLane and Dr. J. E. Ferdinand. He is represented at the Metropolitan Museum of Art by a fine example, the gift to the Museum of Mr. George A. Hearn; at the Long Island Historical Society by a noble canvas, pre-**sented by Mr. George I. Seney;** at the Corcoran and other public galleries by purchases or donations. **In Brooklyn,** so prolific **of fine collections,** examples of Inness are to be found in those of Mr. Henry T. Chapman, Jr., Mr. Edward Olds, Mr. George J. Molloy, and many more. The names of purchasers at the last sales * will furnish further data on this special point.

The location of works owned by collectors of **more remote date** is entirely problematical. Among the artist's earlier patrons were Mr. Thomas Wigglesworth, Mr. Maynard, Mr. Thomas Appleton, of Boston, and ex-Governor Ames, of Massachusetts. Other Boston collectors who owned examples are Mrs. S. D. Warren, Mrs. D. P. Kimball and Mr. O. H. Durell. There is record of pictures by him in the collections of Mr. H. P. Kidder, of Boston, and other New England collectors, but what hands they may now be in, or where, I cannot state. At one time Inness's pictures owed much of their distribution to a curious character of his day, Marcus Spring. Spring belonged to the New England family which produced two notable preachers and religious polemists well known in New York and throughout the country, and was practically the founder of the colony of Eaglewood, **N. J.** He there conducted a military school and formulated the idea upon which our present militia system is based. He was a great admirer of William Page, for whom he built a studio at Eaglewood, and a couple of years later took a fancy to Inness and induced him to settle there. Spring provided the money—or credit—and Inness paid

---

* See appendix.

him in pictures, which Spring disposed of as occasion offered. Some of these Spring pictures come to the surface from time to time, but the artist's significant work was that of his later years. He was not a genius of that class which, having gained its zenith, remains fixed there or falls into declining grooves. His was a fire which age could not wither nor custom stale, and even as time sapped his vital forces he grew ever greater, younger and more powerful in the vital spirit of his art. This is not to cast an aspersion on his works of the Medfield and Eaglewood periods, for they remain worthy of the hand that produced them, but the greatness of an artist must be measured by the organic greatness of his art, and that of George Inness was most powerful and splendid toward the end. He carried to his grave the adherence to and practice of his theory, that it was the duty of every man to himself to live, study, learn, improve and march with his face to the sun when it was declining in the west as steadily as he had faced it when it rose above his horizon.

ADDENDA.

CHARACTERISTICS OF GEORGE INNESS.

GEORGE WILLIAM SHELDON.

(By permission, from THE CENTURY MAGAZINE, *February, 1895.)*

WHAT George Inness most enjoyed, in his hours of ease, was talking and writing on metaphysical subjects like the Darwinian hypothesis of evolution, and the distinction between instinct and reason. He had neither the time nor the inclination to become well read in these matters, but he would wade through a treatise of Archbishop Whately's or John Stuart Mill's, and industriously record the more notable of his animadversions. Certain he was that man could not have descended from the ape, that a brute must always remain a brute, that no class or function could be merged in another class or function. For years he studied the science of numbers—into which Swedenborg also made many incursions—and in several of his manuscripts he demonstrated that the number one represents the infinite; the number two, conjunction; the number three, potency; the number four, substance; the number five, germination; the number six, material condition, and so on. **And wherever** these numbers occurred in the Bible, he was ready, in conversation **or with his pen, to** prove their symbolical significance. So fond was he of these speculations that, had he been rich, he said, he would have pursued them to the exclusion of painting. In reading a manuscript of Inness's it was not always easy to understand his meaning. His sentences were long and involved, and lucidity of expression suffered from haste and inexperience. The art of writing he had never mastered, principally because he never really cared that what he wrote should be read. The extracts from his manuscripts which I have contributed to various periodicals are sometimes obscure in spite of my efforts to get him to explain them. "I don't expect everybody to understand these things," he protested. On one occasion he showed me an essay of perhaps five thousand words, on Zola's "L'Assommoir," in which he had endeavored to prove that this French novel was the greatest temperance tract ever published.

In his conversation, however, especially when answering questions on art matters, he was particularly concise, forcible and clear; and if he had cared to be reported often enough by a competent person, the result might have been a treatise on painting more useful than Leonardo's. I never knew a man whose off-hand thoughts were so well worth preserving; and I never took a stroll with him, or welcomed him at my house, or met him at his own, without wishing that some invisible scribe might make a stenographic report of his talk, and, after submitting it for editorial revision, print it for the benefit of art students.

"A work of art," he said, "is beautiful if the sentiment is beautiful; it is great if the sentiment is vital. Details are to be elaborated only enough to produce the sen-

timent desired. A picture in which the evident intention has been to reach the truth is the picture that the true artist loves. The sleek polish of lackadaisical sentiment, and the puerilities of impossible conditions, are never admirable. Here is a pencil sketch of my own—a young girl about to slip into a brook from the overhanging trunk of a tree. She is entirely disrobed. I made this sketch with the purest kind of motive, feeling that the subject was beautiful, and that in no other way could I convey the sentiment that I had chosen. I shall put it on canvas, keeping the background cool and sweet, and trying to idealize as much as possible. Such a subject, so treated, is as pure as any other. Moreover, I paint the girl at a distance of thirty or forty feet, which gives at once a subdued effect. The mind does not receive the full impression of an object looked at unless this object is viewed at a distance of three times its own length or height; and if it is in the midst of accessories, a proportionate distance should be allowed."

Swedenborgianism interested him as a metaphysical system, especially in its science of correspondences; but he never formulated for himself a theological creed, because, as he said, a man's creed changes with his states of mind, and the formulation made to-day becomes useless to-morrow. He never doubted the immortality of the soul, nor felt that other proof of it was necessary beyond the fact that men generally believe and have believed in immortality. "The consciousness of immortality," he declared, "is wrapped up in all the experiences of my life, and this to me is the end of the argument. Man's unhappiness arises from disobedience to the monitions within him. The principles that underlie art are spiritual principles—the principle of unity and the principle of harmony. Christ never uttered a word that forbade the creating or the enjoying of sensuous form. The fundamental necessity of the artist's life is the cultivation of his moral powers, and the loss of those powers is the loss of artistic power. The efforts of the Catholic Church to excite the imagination of worshippers are admirable, because the imagination is the life of the soul. Art is an essence as subtle as the humanity of God, and, like it, is personal only to love, a stranger to the worldly-minded, a myth to the mere intellect. I would not give a fig for art ideas except as they represent what I, in common with all men, need most—the good of our practice in the art of life. Rivers, streams, the rippling brook, hillsides, sky and clouds, all things that we see, will convey the sentiment of the highest art if we are in the love of God and the desire of the truth."

Sometimes, when feeling a subject deeply, he expressed himself in verse as well as on canvas. A landscape called "Breaking Up," in which storm-clouds were dissolving over the crest of a mountain, an impression dashed off in four hours, suggested to him a poetical "Address of the Clouds to the Earth." Shelley's clouds wandered in thick flocks, shepherded by the unwilling wind. Inness's clouds were brothers, and benefactors of the earth, wooers of the wind that made groves and meadows ring with joyous laughter. In another landscape autumn leaves are falling into a river and floating along toward the sea. Some lines of symbolism describe each leaf as "a little truth from off the tree of life" going to join other truths that had preceded it, and to report progress in the interest of the brotherhood of truths. Rhyme and metre do not count in Inness's poetry. He did not wish them to count.

The hero of a novel of Jane Austen's says: "I like a fine prospect. I do not like crooked, twisted or blasted trees. I admire those that are tall, straight and flourishing. I am not fond of nettles, or thistles, or heath blossoms." One summer afternoon, when Inness and I were walking in Montclair, N. J.,—his home and mine—near the foot of its beautiful mountain, where the "prospect" was particularly fine, the subject that engaged his attention was the delightful gradation of grays in an old rail fence; and on another occasion, when driving down that mountain, from the green slopes of which the trees and cottages of Montclair appear so picturesquely grouped, he feasted his eyes on the rich, creamy tones produced by sunlight shining through the hairs of our gray horse's tail. No natural object was ugly to him. So beautiful was the meanest natural object that no other natural object seemed more beautiful than it. He fondly loved the gnarled writhings of old apple-trees, the affectionate drooping of their branches toward the earth that nourished them, the crooked, twisted olive-trees of Italy, which told stories of man's relations with them. And the landscapes that he painted—civilized landscapes, not savage and untamed— pleased him the most when they most communicated the sentiment of humanity.

In his "Life of Turner," Mr. Hamerton quotes "the following opinion expressed by an intelligent and accomplished American artist, Mr. George Inness:"

"Turner's 'Slave-ship' is the most infernal piece of claptrap ever painted. There is nothing in it. It has as much to do with human affections and thought as a ghost. It is not even a bouquet of color. The color is harsh, disagreeable, discordant.

"These views," says Mr. Hamerton, "while interesting for their frankness, are severe; and their severity is partly due to reaction against Mr. Ruskin's eloquent praises." I remember well the circumstances in which Inness spoke. The "Slave-ship," after having been sold by Mr. Ruskin, had just been removed from New York, where it was coolly received, to Boston, where it became a subject of hot newspaper controversy. I casually asked Inness what he thought of the picture. He expressed himself at once with indignant emphasis and in the most unqualified terms. "But has it no value as color?" I asked. "Not the least in the world," he replied. "Its color is harsh, disagreeable, discordant." Mr. Hamerton is mistaken in supposing that Inness's severity was even partly due to reaction against Ruskin's enthusiastic commendation. Inness was not interested in Ruskin, and nothing occupied him less than the lucubrations of art critics. When he discovered insincerity and falseness in what might have been a great picture, he became angry; he detested insincerity and falseness. Mr. Hamerton admits that the introduction into the canvas of the sharks, the manacles, and the human hand and leg, is so horrible as to revolt him, and that the color is crude.

I have dwelt upon the strength and activity of Inness's intellect, because these qualities produced and explain the beauty of his landscapes. Art, like language, is a means of expressing ideas, and in the work of George Inness the ideas are great and noble. Most of the pictures in the dealers' collections could be described, he thought, by the phrase "intellectual dish-water." "My compositions," said Beethoven, "are not intended to excite the pretty little emotions of women: music ought to strike fire from the soul of a man." This is what Inness's pictures do, and his recreations in theology, poetry and metaphysics are less interesting in themselves than in the evidence they afford of his intellectual power.

His struggle was, while obtaining objective force, not to lose sentiment. He sympathized with Corot, who had had the same struggle, and had confessed himself beaten. He admired Daubigny, because in the struggle Daubigny had been less unsuccessful. He deplored in Meissonier the wilful sacrifice of sentiment to objective force. He considered Millet chiefly as a painter of figures rather than of landscapes, and he thought him the greatest figure-painter that ever lived, because his figures best and most often expressed the tenderest and purest sentiments of labor and of home, with just enough objective force for perfect lucidity. He almost worshipped Rousseau, because, above all other landscape painters, he preserved the local color of trees, of grass and of sky, while maintaining the general tonality of his picture. He had no patience with Cabanel, Bouguereau, Lefebvre, Verboeckhoven and scores of other painters, foreign and native, who, though sought by American collectors, seemed animated by the spirit of commercialism. He believed in objective force, and it was for their lack of it that he criticized the young painters who founded the Society of American Artists, and who had elected him a member of their organization. Speaking of one of their exhibitions, he said, "The poetic quality is not obtained by eschewing any truths or facts of nature which can be included in a harmonious representation;" but at the same time he insisted that men of artistic genius could often dash off an impression which would appeal to the cultivated spectator as more vital than the most laborious efforts of artists less generously endowed.

In his sympathies and his works Inness belonged to the school of Barbizon. As early as 1850 a few of his paintings had found their way to the United States, and Inness was the first American landscapist of distinction to welcome them. He soon went to France to study the methods of Millet, Rousseau, Daubigny and Corot. Millet, then in his thirty-fifth year—Inness was ten years younger—had just abandoned the painting of nude subjects, the sale for which was easy and rapid, and had started upon his unique career as the interpreter of French peasant life. When Inness returned to France, sixteen years later, the Barbizon school was making itself felt. Had he been a Frenchman he would have been recognized as a member of it, with an individuality as distinct as that of Daubigny. At this time he fixed his method of painting, which was as follows: after staining the white canvas with Venetian red, but not enough to lose the sense of transparency, he drew, more or less carefully, with a piece of charcoal, the outlines of the coming picture, and confirmed them with a pencil, putting in a few of the prominent shadows with a little ivory-black on a brush. His principal pigments where white, Antwerp blue, Indian red and lemon chrome. He began anywhere to paint, and worked in mass from generals to particulars, keeping his shadows thin and transparent, and allowing the red with which the canvas was stained to come through as a part of the color. When the pigments were sufficiently dry, he added to his palette cobalt, brown and pink. The last steps were glazing, delicate touching and scumbling.

George Inness had no jealousies and few amusements. He smoked some and took long walks. Often he painted fifteen hours a day. On the dozen or more canvases in his studio he worked as the humor seized him, going from one to another with palette and maul-stick, and always standing when painting. He had two styles, one restrained, the other impetuous; and as he grew older the latter prevailed. Correctness of linear design was less important than color, atmosphere and chiaroscuro; but first in importance was the resolve to convey distinctly the impressions of a personal, vital force. Believing that he obtained with oils all the delicacy of watercolors, and much strength in addition, he did not paint in water-colors. His sincerity, his faith, his earnestness—all that which escapes like a perfume from his works—increased with his years, and with the honorable fame and competence that he had earned. One of his landscapes is called "Light Triumphant"—a name that fitly described them all.

A Reminiscence of George Inness.

ELLIOTT DAINGERFIELD.*

(*By permission, from* The Monthly Illustrator, *March, 1895.*)

TO a young man in any of the professions it is an event of no little importance when he is brought into close contact with one who has already achieved fame, and the loftiest position his profession offers. It was with a certain exaltation, a quickened hopefulness, that I met George Inness in the early days of '85, when his own power was reaching its summit, and his works were glowing with that unusual lustre which makes them the most dignified efforts in American Art.

When, for the first few weeks of my acquaintance, he failed to remember me—even the very name was lost to him—there was in my mind no sense of resentment. One with quick perception could readily see that Inness had no interest in the external man—he was often unconscious of himself: the real *ego* was that great striving quantity unseen with eyes, the soul, the heart, the brain of a man, and through the expressions of these, only, could he discover himself or recognize the individuality in another. Day after day I went into his studio, only two doors removed from my own, and there, watching the progress of numerous canvases in silence, and with the sort of reverence one must feel in the presence of genius, grew up a knowledge of the man and the mighty engine of his mind, its purposes and achievements, which will ever remain a heritage of strength in the struggles of my own life.

Invincible is perhaps the one word which defines George Inness's character. Arrogant, he has been called, but falsely; egotistical, selfish, and all the other phrases that unsuccessful jealous minds usually apply to those who are intolerant of false effort, and falser success, in the fields where alone Truth is the aim and Truth the goal. Never once, in all my long acquaintance with him, have I known Inness satisfied with a work of his own. Times without number I have seen a new light flash in his eye; a quick, eager toss of the head and thrusting back of the hair, when some problem with which he had been struggling for days or months—perhaps years—was yielding under the sway of his fierce energy; then it was he gave vent to

---

* Elliott Daingerfield is an American artist of great merit, born at Harpers Ferry, Va., in 1859. In 1880 he came to New York to study art, and during the same year made his first exhibit at the National Academy. He worked in water-colors and in oil, confining himself to simple subjects and building up his method out of study and experiment upon the basis of nature. To the discreet eye, the sincere feeling and growing force of his work was full of a promise which the artist has amply fulfilled. He has recently developed a productiveness of a high order of sentiment and feeling, with forcible and harmonious color, and an original and decided technique. His pictures possess the poetic quality in an eminent degree. Mr. Daingerfield was for several years a neighbor of George Inness in the studio building in West Fifty-fifth street, New York, and was a great favorite with the veteran.

those expressions of satisfaction which have **been** called conceit; but, mark you, when the morning came, or the new mood, be that canvas never so fine, if one thing there jarred on the man's artistic sensibility he attacked it with all the old enthusiasm, with a dogged determination to bring it to his own high standard.

This spirit absolves him forever from all charges of vanity. The pleading of friends, artists or buyers availed nothing. His creed was ever to make his work more perfect; and it is a truth well attested that, however beautiful the first attempt might have been, the completed work was almost always the finer. It was in such struggles that Inness conquered his limitations and grew into the powerful, virile and poetic painter we now see him.

His **moods were** so well known to me that I could readily tell from his very knock at my door whether I was to be taken off across the hall to his studio to view some great advance in his picture, or whether he was to drop into a chair in silence for a while, worn, tired, and with that depression of spirit which only the artistic nature can understand. At such a time, one word upon some abstract theme, no matter what, if really serious, would stir him into life and intense speech. It would not be argument, as between two; for, when Inness talked, the flame needed no draught. It blazed and flared until his own conclusions were reached, and then faded, even as the glow on some of his own forest trees seems to fade in the twilight time, until the deep silence left no room for speech. Nor were his arguments always carried to logical sequence: what mattered it? Does the storm forever sweep across the exact field you or I have chosen for its path? The rush and go of it were all there and the interest. If there were sympathy, which means understanding, in the listener's soul, these monologues of his yielded many great truths to him.

He came into my studio one day, with all the unrest and nervous eagerness which characterized him when thinking intensely, threw out several sentences about his picture, his purpose in it, etc., then with a sort of mad rush he said:

"What's it all about? What does it mean—this striving—this everlasting painting, painting, painting away one's life? What is Art? That's the question I've been asking myself, and I've answered it this way:" (I drew a writing-pad to me, and jotted down his words; they are worth thinking about oftener than once.) "Art is the endeavor on the part of Mind (Mind being the creative faculty) to express, through the senses, ideas of the great principles of unity."

Perhaps no more characteristic sentence has ever been recorded of him. It satisfied him. He had made his conclusion and expressed it. He did not propose to supply us with brains to understand what the "principles of unity" may be. We might struggle as we pleased with that problem, as perhaps he had struggled with the other, although to a tyro the last seems exactly the same as the first. Art, Religion and the Single Tax Theory were his chief themes, and, by a curiously interesting weaving, his logic could make all three one and the same thing.

Oblivious to externals, both of persons and things, he often said and did much that evoked harsh criticism, but at heart, it may be truthfully said, he was as gentle as a child, even tender, and swiftly sympathetic. What a delight it was to watch him paint in one of those impetuous moods which so often possessed him. The colors were almost never mixed—he had his blue theories, black, umber, and in earlier days bitumen: he even had an orange-chrome phase. With a great mass of color he attacked the canvas, spreading it with incredible swiftness, marking in the great masses with a skill and method all his own, and impossible to imitate; here, there, all over the canvas, rub, rub, dig, scratch, until the very brushes seemed to rebel, spreading their bristles as fiercely as they did in the days of yore along the spine of their porcine possessor.

34

But stand here, fifteen feet away. What a marvelous change is there! A great rolling billowy cloud sweeping across the blue expanse, graded with such subtle skill over the undertone. Vast trees with sunlight flecking their trunks, meadows, ponds—mere suggestions, but beautiful; foregrounds filled with detail, where there had been no apparent effort to produce it, delicate flowers scratched in with the thumb-nail or handle of the brush. One's imagination was so quickened **that it** supplied all the finish needed.

Inness used to say that his forms were at the tips of his fingers, just as the alphabet was at the end of the tongue. Surely it was true, and when he "struck a snag," as he called it, and he almost always did (I used to think sometimes for the fun of the struggle that was to follow), 'twas in the *construction* of his picture, not in any mere matter of painting. He would find out where the "hitch" was, and then go on.

Under excitement of this kind he could do most astounding things. One morning a frame came in which had been mismeasured; he sent for a canvas to fit it, rapidly sketched in a composition, and produced one of the most limpid, lovely pieces of pure sunlight I have ever seen him paint. But, alas! he said there was a "hitch," and subsequent labor transformed it—one of the rare cases when I wish "well enough" had been let alone.

I once had the good fortune to paint a little picture that pleased him; he caught sight of it lying on the floor against the wall, and exclaimed:

"Hello, who did that?"

I told him. Stooping down he caught it up, pushed his glasses far back on his head, and examined it, with many expressions that I remember with deep satisfaction, put it down and walked out of the room. The next morning he came in again, and, taking up the picture, asked: "What do you expect to get for that?" I mentioned a price, thinking he meant to advise some one to buy it, but he answered at once, "I'll take it," walked to the desk, and made out a check.

Then, as if he meant to aid me still farther up the hill, he caught up my palette and brushes, and for an hour painted at a figure picture, which I had thought finished, to show me "how" it ought to be done. I have never touched **that picture.** It remains a souvenir of the day I had my biggest lesson in art, and I value and feel the importance of every word he then said.

It was not always, however, that he was so interested or so complimentary. Years after I undertook a picture which had a line of rail-fence running down to the foreground; he saw it and objected somewhat to the arrangement. I undertook to argue the point, and said, "Why can't I have it that way, if it pleases me?" "So you can," was his answer, "if you want to be a d—d idiot." I changed the fence.

So incident upon incident might be multiplied of this strange, erratic, always artistic nature, that forever lived at white heat, unveiling in vast waves his visions of color, tone and grandeur of line, until we were drawn nearer to the nature he loved, and in his art perceived the earnest seeker after Truth.

With the works of all the great painters he had a profound acquaintance, and an analytical as well as synthetic knowledge. His admiration for the really great results was sincere and often enthusiastic. For the evanescent, soap-bubble **successes** in art he had no toleration, and with a force quite irresistible he pointed out the fallacy in efforts which were the result of mere skill, or a certain jugglery in color, brush-work, or what not. "Limitation there must be in art," he would say; "how hopeless it all seems when we look at nature."

For Titian, Angelo, Raphael, Rembrandt and many others of the great men he was unstinting in praise. To make a landscape as perfect in its unity as a portrait by Rembrandt was an ever-present ideal. Rousseau, Millet, Corot, Constable, Turner and Claude he quoted often as being at the head of the list, and, perceiving their faults, as he often did, their merits never escaped him. Of the great Englishman he said hard things for his brutality and "stupidity," although to certain works, such as the "Pier at Calais," he gave unlimited praise. As his own ideals were high, so was his condemnation of all failure or frivolity of intention severe, often bitter, but not unjust.

No reminiscence of Inness would be complete without some mention of his great power as a colorist, for all his philosophy, all his many-sided nature, seemed to express itself in the fulness and beauty of color. We are not to make comparisons with the work of others; that were needless—Inness's color was his own. The early morning, with its silver, tender tones, offered him as great opportunity for the expression of what he called "fulness of color" as did the open glare of the noonday or the fiery bursts of sunset. Mention has been made of his different color-moods, and one fairly held the breath to see him spread with unrelenting fury a broad scumble of orange-chrome over the most delicate, subtle, gray effect, in order to get more "fulness;" and still more strange was it to see, by a mysterious technical use of black or blue, the same tender silver morning unfold itself, but stronger, firmer, fuller in its tone quality. "One must use pure color," he would say; "the picture must be so constructed that the 'local' of every color can be secured, whether in the shadow or the light." Many of his canvases are criticised because of an over-greenness or an intensity of the blues, but deeper study shows the man's principle, for which he strove with the whole force of his nature—a perfect balance of color quality everywhere in the picture. The mass of offending green will be found to balance perfectly with the mass of gray or blue of the sky. So that the whole canvas, viewed with that perceptive power without which there is no justice in either the criticism or the critic, becomes an harmonious balance. With all the intensity of his powerful palette, Inness maintained that the "middle tone" was the secret of all success in color—he strove for it until the end, and so great was his effort that the latest works are but waves of wonderful color, marvelous and mysterious—the very essence of the beauty of nature. When he chose to put aside his theories and produce a "tone study," following the habit of those masters who have glorified modern French art, he was as subtle as any of them and far less labored; but it is in his very intensity that he has preserved his individuality, and if we are to understand him aright we must study him from his own standpoint. In his earlier life his drawing was precise and accurate to a wonderful degree, being elaborated to the very verge of the horizon.

In the beginning Inness strove for knowledge with most untiring effort. His early pictures are full of intricate, elaborate detail; 'twas thus he gained that knowledge of forms which put them at his finger-tips. Always, however, there was the largeness of perception which enabled him to understand masses, and divide his compositions into just proportions of light and shade; and under all one saw the poet and the philosopher. Painfully objective as were these early efforts, they were tasks along the great highway which at last led him to those heights whence he saw and understood the *subjective* in nature and expressed it in his art.

Analytical, profoundly so, when he chose to be, with increasing years his art grew more and more synthetic, and the very latest works are most so of all, and strangely beautiful in the total elimination of needless detail and sure grasp of *idea*. His art became at that time a sort of soul-language, which, if you have not the speech, you may not understand, but it is none the less beautiful. To-day we are at too near a view. Let us await the coming years; he will then need no defense.

GEORGE INNESS'S OPINIONS.

(From " A Painter on Painting," in HARPER'S MAGAZINE *for* February, 1878.)

SOME artists like a short brush to paint with and others a long brush; some want a smooth canvas and others a rough canvas; some a canvas with a hard surface and others a canvas with an absorbent surface; some a white canvas and others a stained canvas. Decamps, you know, bought old pictures and painted over them; his canvas was a painting before he touched it; and I should say that if a man wished to paint as Delacroix painted, an old picture would suit him as well as a new canvas **to put his scene on. On the other** hand, Couture painted only over a fresh, clean canvas, slightly stained, while Troyon evidently preferred a plain, **white** surface, because **he** and Couture used transparent washes of color, through which the original surface **of** their canvases could often be seen. But Delacroix painted solid all through, and his quality, unlike that of Troyon, Couture, Ziem and other artists, does not depend upon the transparency of his color. Some artists use quick-drying oils for varnishing, and others slow-drying oils. Most artists prefer to paint in a north room, because there the light is more equable—the sun does not come in. But Mr. Page likes a south room, although I don't know why. You **see there are no** absolute rules about methods of painting.

* * *

Pupils can't be taught much by an artist. I have found that explanations usually hinder them, or else make their work stereotyped. If I had a pupil in my studio, I should say to him, as Troyon once said in similar circumstances: "Sit down and paint." Still, now and then I should tell him a principle of light and shade, of color, or of *chiaro-oscuro*, and criticise his work, showing him where he was right and where he was wrong, as if I were walking with him through a gallery of pictures, and pointing out their faults and their merits. The best way to teach art is the Paris way. There the pupils—two, three or more—hire a room, hire their models and set up their easels. Once or twice a week the master comes in, looks at their work, and makes suggestions and remarks, advising the use of no particular method, but leaving each pupil's individuality free. If a young man paints regularly in the studio of his teacher, he is apt to lose spontaneity and vitality, and to become a dead reproduction of his teacher. Van Marcke suffered, I think, from this cause. He painted within arm's length of Troyon, and he has become a sort of inanimate Troyon.

* * *

Meissonier is a very wonderful painter, but his aim seems to be a material rather than a spiritual one. The imitative has too strong a hold upon his mind; hence, even in his simplest and best things, we find the presence of individualities which should have been absent. Even in his greatest efforts there is not that power to awaken our emotion which the simplest works of a painter like Decamps possess. There every detail of the picture is a part of the vision which impressed the artist, and which he purposed to reproduce to the end that it might impress others; and every detail has been subordinated to the expression of the artist's impression. Take one of his pictures, "The Suicide" *—a representation of a dead man lying on a bed in a garret, partly in the sunlight. All is given up to the expression of the idea of *desolation*. The scene is painted as though the artist had seen it in a dream. Nothing is done to gratify curiosity or to withdraw the mind from the great central point—the dead man; yet all is felt to be complete and truly finished. The spectator carries away **from it a** strong impression, but his memory is not taxed with a multitude of facts. The simple story is impressed upon his mind and remains there forever. Contrast such a work with a Meissonier. Here the tendency seems to me to be toward the gratification of lower desires, and you see long-winded processions and reviews; great historical compositions; you see horses painted with nails in their shoes, and men upon them with buttons on their coats—nails and buttons at distances from the spectator where they could not be seen by any eye, however sharp or disciplined. Gérome is worse than Meissonier, and in the same way. So is Detaille; so are the multitudes of their school. It is the same story all through. Decamps' mind is more perfectly governed by an original impulse, and it **obeys more** perfectly the laws of vision.

* * *

As landscape painters I consider Rousseau, Daubigny and Corot among the very best. Daubigny, particularly, and Corot, have mastered the relation of things in nature, one to the other, and have attained in their greatest works representations more or less nearly perfect. But in their day the science underlying impressions was not fully known. The advances already made in that science, united to the knowledge of the principles underlying the attempts made by these artists, will, we may hope, soon bring the art of landscape painting to perfection. Rousseau was perhaps the greatest French landscape painter; but I have seen in this country some of the smaller things of Corot which appeared to me to be truly and thoroughly spontaneous representations of nature, although weak in their key of color, as Corot always is. But his idea was a pure one, and he had long been a hard student. Daubigny also had a pure idea, and so had Rousseau. There was no affectation about these men; there were no tricks of color.

* * *

Parts of Turner's pictures are splendid specimens of realization, but their effect is spoiled by other parts, which are full of falsity and claptrap. Very rarely, if ever, does Turner give the impression of the real that nature gives. For example, in that well-known work in the London National Gallery, which presents a group of fishing boats between the spectator and the sun (the sun in a fog), we find that half of the picture, if cut out by itself, would be most admirable. Into the other half, however, he has introduced a dock, some fishermen, some fishes: an accumulation of small things impossible under the circumstances to unity of vision. Frequently, as in this case, in fact, almost continually, the sun is represented as before us, and objects are introduced for the purpose of conveying Turner's ideal of effects in all sorts of false lights, as though there were half a dozen different suns shining from various positions in the heavens. Of course, all this may appeal—as probably he intended it should—to foolish fancies, which are only sensuous weaknesses and not the offspring of pro-

---

* Now in the Walters' collection, at Baltimore, Md.

found feeling. Turner was a man of very great genius, but of perverted powers—
perverted by love of money, of the world, or of something or other. His best things
are his marines, in which appear great dramatic power. Constable was the first
English painter of the modern landscape idea; and the French school, to which
Troyon, Corot, Daubigny and others I have mentioned belong, was founded upon him.
These Frenchmen learned from Constable and improved upon him. But in Turner,
the dramatic predominated—the desire to tell a story. I think the general estimate
that any true artist must form before the works of Turner is that he was a very
subtle scene-painter. He stands alone, it is true, and I do him all reverence; but his
genius was not of the highest order.

* * *

Our country is flooded **with** the mercantile imbecilities of Verboeckhoven and
hundreds of other **European** artists whose very names are a detestation to any lover
of truth. The skin-deep beauties of Bouguereau and others of whom he is a type,
are a loathing to those who hate the idolatry which worships waxen images. The
true artist loves only that work in which the evident intention has been to attain the
truth, and such work is not easily brought to a fine polish. What he hates is that
which has evidently been painted for a market. The sleekness of which we see so
much in pictures is a result of spiritual inertia, and is his detestation. It is simply a
mercantile finish. Who ever thinks about Michael Angelo's work being finished?
No great artist ever finished a picture or a statue. It is mercantile work that is
finished, and finish is what the picture dealers cry for. Instead of covering the wall
of his mansion with works of character, or, what is better, with those works of inspiration which allure the mind to the regions of the unknown, he is apt to cover
them with the sleek polish of lackadaisical sentiment, or the puerilities of impossible
conditions. Consequently the picture dealer, although he may have, or may have
had, something of the artistic instinct, is overwhelmed by commercial necessity.
The genuine artist sometimes supposes that he suffers because his love is not of the
world. But let him beware of such a fancy. It is a ghost. It has no reality. Our
unhappinesses arise from disobedience to the monitions within us. **Let** every endeavor be honest, and although the results of our labors may often **seem** abortive,
there will here and there flash out from them a spark of truth which shall gain us the
sympathy of a noble spirit.

* * *

The true use of art is, first, to cultivate the artist's own spiritual nature, and
secondly, to enter as a factor in general civilization. And the increase of these
effects depends upon the purity of the artist's motive in the pursuit of art. Every
artist who, without reference to external circumstances, aims truly to represent the
ideas and emotions which come to him when he is in the presence of nature, is in
process of his own spiritual development, and is a benefactor of his race. No man
can attempt **the** reproduction of any idea within him, from a pure motive or love of
the idea itself, without being in the course of his own regeneration. The difficulties
necessary to be overcome in communicating the substance of his idea (which, in this
case, is feeling or emotion) to the end that the idea may be more and more perfectly
conveyed to others, involve the exercise of his intellectual faculties; and soon the
discovery is made that the moral element underlies all, that unless the moral also is
brought into play the intellectual faculties are not in condition for conveying the
artistic impulse or inspiration. The mind may, indeed, be convinced of the means of
operation, but only when the moral powers have been cultivated do the conditions
exist necessary to the transmission of the artistic inspiration which is from truth and
goodness itself. Of course no man's motive can be absolutely pure and single. His

environment affects him. But the true artistic impulse is divine. The reality of every artistic vision lies in the thought animating the artist's mind. This is proven by the fact that every artist who attempts only to imitate what he sees fails to represent that something which comes home to him as a satisfaction, fails to make a representation corresponding in the satisfaction felt in his first perception. Consequently we find that men of strong artistic genius, which enables them to dash off an impression coming, as they suppose, from what is outwardly seen, may produce a work, however incomplete or imperfect in details, of greater vitality, having more of the peculiar quality called "freshness," either as to color or spontaneity of artistic impulse, than can other men after laborious efforts—a work which appeals to the cultivated mind as sometimes more or less perfect of nature. Now this spontaneous movement by which he produces a picture is governed by the law of homogeneity or unity, and accordingly we find that in proportion to the perfection of his genius is the unity of his picture. The highest art is where has been most perfectly breathed the sentiment of humanity. Rivers, streams, the rippling brook, the hillside, the sky, clouds—all things that we see—can convey that sentiment if we are in the love of God and the desire of truth. Some persons think that landscape has no power of communicating human sentiment. But this is a great mistake. The civilized landscape peculiarly can, and therefore I love it more and think it more worthy of reproduction than that which is savage and untamed. It is more significant. Every act of man, everything of labor, effort, suffering, want, anxiety, necessity, love, marks itself wherever it has been. In Italy, I remember frequently noticing the peculiar ideas that came to me from seeing odd-looking trees that had been used, or tortured, or twisted—all telling something about humanity. American landscape, perhaps, is not so significant; but still everything in nature has something to say to us. No artist need fear that his work will not find sympathy if he only works earnestly and lovingly.

OPINIONS ON GEORGE INNESS.

INNESS paints at times with haste and carelessness; he does not always do himself justice. Yet rarely do we see one of his landscapes without finding there is a picturesque effect or a subtle meaning, indicative of the rarest skill and the most absolute genius; if limited in scope, yet actual and true.

—TUCKERMAN, "Book of the Artists."

* * *

Wildly unequal and eccentric as Inness is, recklessly experimentative, indulging in sameness of ideas, often destroying good work by bad, lawless in manner, using pigments, sometimes, as though they were mortar and he a plasterer, still there is ever perceptible in his works imagination, feeling and technical instinct of a high order. The French school has tempered his style; but he is by no means a mechanical follower of it. He can be as sensitive as he is powerful in his rendering of nature's phenomena. Inness gives with equal felicity the drowsy heat, hot shimmer and languid quiet of a summer's noon, or the storm-weighed atmosphere, its dark masses of vapor and the wild gathering of thunderclouds with their solemn hush before **the** tempest breaks. He uses sunlight sparingly, but it glows **on** his **canvas** and **turns** darkness into hope and joy.

—J. J. JARVIS, "The Art Idea."

* * *

The influence of the French school of landscape art is probably more strongly apparent in George Inness than in the pictures of any other American painter, and yet he is no imitator, although the more subtle features of this idea may be detected in all of his pictures. There is no American artist who has acquired greater fame as such than George Inness, neither can we recall any who is so varied in his moods. . . . In his happy moods he has painted some of the best landscape pictures ever produced in this country.

Art Journal, March, 1876.

* * *

At a time when the making of what we are called upon to accept as landscapes has become a trick, at the command of any half-trained amateur, and when it has become a species of manufacture with a great majority of the class of painters who call themselves professional; at a time when dexterity of technique on the one hand, eccentricity on the other, and mere prettiness as a third wheel to the coach, trundle their way gayly along the highway of art, leaving no record that will survive their passage, there is something infinitely majestic in the presence of a man, gray with years of tireless struggle, and spurred by a long life of self-criticism, striding steadily forward on unfaltering feet, making the great work of to-day but a step upward toward the greater work of to-morrow, seeking his ideal of nature with his face turned to the sun. No higher honor could be accorded to George Inness, nearing three score and ten, with the fire of youth still burning within him, and the light of truth still shining in his undimmed eyes, than to make note with wonder that his progress continues, as if he had conquered the secret of outrunning time, and that his art grows steadily more sovereign in its power, long past the period where in the common course of nature the artist's sun reaches its zenith and commences its decline. Born in 1825, upon the very dawn of landscape art in America, Mr. Inness stands to-day in its splendid noon in the creation of whose most dazzling radiance his brush has been the necromancer's wand. He set out upon the journey on uncertain feet. **Born at** Newburgh, N. Y., apprenticed to a steel engraver, and compelled to **give the work** up by illness, a few lessons from Regis Gignoux and his own genius constituted his entire artistic capital. Physical maladies and poverty beset his feeble steps. Without a guide, at a time when even the guides were little better than blind themselves, he battled his way onward and upward, surviving failures and retrieving errors, until he found the turning of the road that led to the light. His whole life has been an experiment upon himself. His first visit to Europe, in 1850, began the work of mental organization. The progress of his developments is clearly denoted in his works. Working without masters and without schools, he made the best art he could find provide him with advice, and made nature herself the school in which the lessons might be applied. Never satisfied with himself, he never remained stationary in his art, and his powers have not ceased to ripen. His art is an art of revelations, because he finds in nature a variety which is endless and a new problem to succeed every problem already solved. The series of pictures which constitute his record of American landscape, and which form the crowning productions of his career, are part of our national chronicles as well as masterpieces of our national art. In his studio at Montclair, among the Orange Mountains, he is writing history with his brush as surely as a Prescott or a Bancroft ever wrote it with their pens.

—Catalogue of the Thos. B. Clarke Collection, Philadelphia, 1891.

* * *

Inness paints nature as the Ossian of the Highlands sang of it—in its great outer rather than in its little inner form.

Henry Eckford, in *The Century* Magazine for May, 1882.

* * *

George Inness presented himself in Germany for the first time in 1892. To his later years belong his most significant productions. His life was, like Corot's, an incessant advance and renewal. Once he is broad and powerful, like Rousseau; again tender and poetic like Corot, here idyllically pastoral like Daubigny, there pathetic and brooding like Dupré. All his pictures are broadly painted, deeply felt, and full-souled symphonies of tone. The history of art must welcome him as one of the most varied and finest landscape painters of the century.

—Richard Muther, "Geschichte der Malerei im Neunzehnten Jahrhundert."

* * *

When I came to this country for the first time, in 1890, I had the pleasure and honor to form an acquaintance with George Inness, who received me at his country house in a most charming manner, and showed me all the landscapes he had then on his easels. Some of these I see again to-day, after his lamented demise, and, being urged by a friend to write a few lines, as I had previously done, in 1890, in the *New York Times*, about the exhibition of Mr. Richard H. Halsted's collection of Inness's works at the American Art Galleries, I am willing to act as a critic of art, provided painters may be allowed to write on painting. Perhaps I may be permitted to do so, once in a while at any rate, if it be only to please a friend and myself. The moral and physical personality of George Inness has made a last impression on my mind. He was naturally nervous, impressionable, sensitive to the richness of coloring, to its enamel, to its material, as well as sensitive to the poetical and quick effects of nature. Living as he was, in the very midst of the latter, looking about its **grandeur, its** marvels of light, he especially liked the evenings of autumn, the **autumn of his na-**tive country. He brought out of it powerful works, full of emotion and painted in a rutilant color. He was always careful, however, to retain for oil painting its special qualities of material and enamel, and never tried to put the essential qualities of either pastel or water-colors into oil painting. Thus, he was proceeding from Millet, Jules Dupré and **Rousseau, while** preserving his original mark. We always proceed from the time **in** which we live and the works that have impressed us at the beginning **of our career, but** our personality comes out. **however.** Baudry and Chavannes, in their decorative works, proceeded from the Italian masters of the fifteenth and six-teenth centuries, although in a different degree; the English school of the beginning of this century had influence over Delacroix. A new art cannot be born in a day; a whole century is hardly sufficient for it. But I must speak now of the works that I like best among Mr. Halsted's collection of Inness's works. No. 7 would, if signed by Turner, Millet or Corot, be worth $10.000 and over. In my view it is equivalent to the best landscape ever painted by any great landscape painter. No warm and stormy day in June has ever been felt better nor expressed better. Nature has been sometimes seen as if it were asleep in a golden atmosphere, when there was no wind, but an oppressive air full of languor; the sun behind the clouds was not throwing **any** shade under the trees; waters were still in the shallow rivers, one could feel that not a single leaf was trembling. Nature was taking her afternoon's nap. Now, in my opinion, Inness, as I remember him, must have had such a feeling when he painted that magnificent piece of art, which is undoubtedly of the highest order. The color-ing of the green tones is positively delightful, for it may be said that no eye was **ever** more sensitive than Inness's to the richness of the green tones brought about **by the** summer light. This painting should be at the Metropolitan Museum **of Art. No.** 20 is " brother " **to** No. 7, and shows the same skill in coloring the strong light and **storms** of summer. The coloring of this souvenir of a storm in summer is really ex-quisite. Turner has never brought together his remembrances of a day like this with more richness of material or a more observing mind. No. 3 is a continuation of a series that is a real apotheosis of the sun. No. 15 shows white green tones in a gray, rainy sky, forerunner of a storm, which are enameled in a surprisingly artistic man-ner. The symphony of the green tones, supported and accompanied by the gray clouds, is masterly scored. No. 6 is a good painting, and so is No. 13. These lines are but brief homage to true talent. When the time comes—and it will come, sooner or later—to do full justice to George Inness, I shall be glad to have been one of the first, perhaps, who felt an artistic emotion in contemplating these paintings, that so clearly show the impressionability of a thorough artist, a lover of nature and an executor of rare merit.

BENJAMIN CONSTANT, in the *New York Times*, 1895

THE GEORGE INNESS SALE.

(*From* THE COLLECTOR, *Feb. 15, 1895.*)

THE executors' sale of the pictures of the late George Inness is a sale of record. It is the only one we have had in the United States which approaches the importance of the post-mortem sales of Corot, Millet, Troyon and the other great French painters. There has been no approximation to it excepting in the disposition, also by Messrs. Ortgies & Co., of the pictures left by Alexander H. Wyant, the result of which was given in full in *The Collector* for Feb. 15, 1894. The grandeur of the artist, the peculiar **interest** of the man, and the now general appreciation of his greatness, render **the Inness sale a just** tribute. To collectors the figures here given should prove **of interest,** even if they do not yet own examples of our foremost landscape painter, and of value if they do. The sale comprises the entire works of Mr. Inness to be sold by the estate, so that its results may be accepted as a standard upon which to base future calculations. The prices are given seriatim, in order of sale as catalogued. The total was over $108,000.

Out of my Studio Door, Montclair, 12x14, 1878. John D. Crimmins	$250
In the Catskills, 12x14, 1860. S. D. Warren	300
Durham, Conn., 16x24, 1879. Edward M. Colie	250
Edge of the Wood, 16x24, 1866. George R. Green	300
Pequonic River, Pompton, 11x13½, 1877. F. M. Shepard	210
Perugia, Italy, 18½x11, 1873. Mrs. F. S. Fisher	200
Pompton, 10x13, 1877. S. C. Van Deusen	135
Back of the Old Barn, 12x18, 1888. Francis T. Lloyd	300
Leeds, New York, 9½x13, 1864. P. H. McMahon	200
Niagara, 16x24, 1885. Henry Hess, Jr.	320
Albano, Italy, 9½x13½, 1872. H. J. Luce	110
Artists' Brook, North Conway, 16x24, 1875. Henry Sampson	500
Leeds, New York, 12x18, 1864. M. Merriam	230
Summer Evening, Montclair, New Jersey, 30x45, 1892. Mrs. W. R. Linn	1,000
Light House, Nantucket, 18x26, 1879. A. H. Alker	500
Old Oak, Lyndhurst, New Forest, England, 25x30, 1887. C. H. De Silver	1,675
Hastings, New York, 16x18½, 1868. A. H. Alker	120
Early Morning, Montclair, New Jersey, 30x45, 1892. E. W. Bass	900
Lake Nemi, Italy, 18x26, 1872. D. B. Samuels	225
The Brook, 8x10, 1876. S. C. Van Deusen	110
The Hermit, 12x18, 1885. C. L. Hutchinson	175
Winter at Montclair, New Jersey, 22x36, 1884. E. W. Bass	200

47

Looking over the Hudson at Milton, 27x22, 1888. A. S. Lascell................ $475
The Pond, 29x37½. Louis Ettlinger.. 460
A Stormy Day, 22x28. Wm. Macbeth.. 475
Eventide, Tarpon Springs, Florida, 30x45, 1893. H. E. Hayes................. 750
Near my Studio, Milton, 20x30, 1882. W. A. White.......................... 390
Autumn, 20x30, 1892. G. E. Tewksbury.. 300
Sunrise, 30x45, 1891. W. A. White... 1,200
After the Shower, 20x30, 1886. W. V. Lawrence............................. 210
Hillside, 20x30. M. A. Ryerson.. 575
A Breezy Day, 22x27, 1893. S. P. Avery, Jr.................................... 950
Autumn, 25x30, 1892. S. P. Avery, Jr.. 775
St. Andrews, New Brunswick, 1893. J. C. Wells............................. 1,125
Coast of Cornwall. W. Barbour.. 750
Late Sunset, 39x53. G. E. Tewksbury... 950
The Red Oaks, 36x54, 1894. Chas. E. Clark.................................. 1,025
The Coming Storm, 60x120, 1892...Withdrawn

Among the purchasers at the sale may be noted Messrs. Charles L. Hutchinson,
Cyrus J. McCormick and Martin A. Ryerson, of Chicago; Mrs. S. D. Warren, of
Boston; Messrs. John D. Crimmins, Edward Kearney, G. E. Tewksbury, Frederic
Bonner, A. W. Drake, Joseph Hartley, M. Arnheim, Thomas B. Clarke, L. G. Bloom-
ingdale, C. C. Ruthrauff, David McCosker, Louis Ellinger, J. S. Wood, P. H.
McMahon, G. A. Hobart, F. S. Wells, F. J. Smith, B. F. Luckey, J. Falk, L. C. Earl,
Charles M. Kurtz, G. C. Riggs, J. O'Connor, S. L. G. Watkins, E. M. Collis, J. H.
Dougherty, G. N. Miller, F. S. Weeks, S. R. Metcalf, R. E. Shirmer, W. T. Sander,
Edward Thaw, W. C. Clark, F. L. Fisher, Allan Marquand, W. T. Covington, W.
Sherburne, F. M. Shepherd, F. S. Fisher, Henry Hess, Jr., H. J. Luce, A. H. Alker,
D. B. Samuels, Carl H. De Silver, John Notman, F. L. Leland, F. J. Briggs, C. S.
Schultz, S. E. Buchanan, John R. Watters, F. H. Scott, Graham Lusk, John T. Barnes,
W. N. Peak, Mrs. F. H. Bosworth, C. H. Houghton, R. K. Mygatt, F. L. Babbitt, J.
M. Martin and James A. Ross, the latter of Montreal. Purchases were also made for
the Century Association and the Union League Club, of New York.

There is, in connection with this sale, a point to be noted of much interest to
collectors. A month before Messrs. Ortgies & Co. made the executors' sale, at
Chickering Hall, the American Art Association sold the Inness collection of Mr.
Richard H. Halsted, in their galleries on Madison Square. The Halsted collection
numbered twenty pictures, all of a high and many of the first order. The sale had,
apparently, been decided on by Mr. Halsted in consequence of the very extensive
advertising which the executors' collection had received from its exhibition at the
Fine Arts Building, previous to its transfer to the galleries of Ortgies & Co. The
general opinion at the time was that it would suffer from antedating the executors'
sale, which, being final, and disposing of everything of the artist's in his possession
at his death, would, in its way, afford a scale of prices which would be authoritative.
It was argued that, valuable as the Halsted pictures were, people would wait to see
whether those belonging to the estate were not more valuable, and to ascertain what
prices they would reach; that, in short, the Halsted sale would not create an
enthusiasm among collectors or bring out the buyers, because it was premature. At
the executors' sale the smaller pictures—say, on an average, from 14x30 to 20x30
inches—brought more than they would have done at private sale, and many of them
were studies rather than pictures in the conventional acceptance of the terms. The
Halsted pictures, all of a market standard, and purchased by Mr. Halsted at full

prices, **were at** the most moderate estimate of experts appraised at $40,000—which was about what he had paid for them, with the legal interest which is supposed to accrue upon an investment. These facts being held in mind, the following correct report of the Halsted sale is not only interesting in itself, but valuable as showing the close business discrimination which collectors, and even casual buyers of pictures, make in their purchases of works under the hammer. The Halsted sale is given as catalogued, with the names of the buyers, and shows, as will be noted, a deficiency of nearly $9,000 on the expert's appraisals **of** its value and on its actual cost to its owner.

"Autumn Gold," J. R. Watters	$1,650
"The Edge of the Forest," C. W. Gould	1,450
"Sunset on the Passaic," J. R. Watters	1,175
"The Coming Shower," E. Thaw	1,050
"Twilight in Florida," J. H. Schiff	1,100
"Tenafly Oaks," E. Thaw	2,100
"Valley of the Olive Oaks," W. M. Laffan	1,600
"A Breezy Autumn," Mrs. C. F. Butterfield	1,450
"Summer Foliage," T. B. Clarke	1,050
"A Woodland Path," J. R. Watters	750
"The Clearing," E. Thaw	1,750
"Midsummer," A. T. White	1,450
"An Autumn Sunset," Louis Ettlinger	1,200
"Sunrise," W. A. Putnam	1,300
"Passing Storm," Mrs. Butterfield	2,150
"Near the Village—October," Franklin Murphy	1,400
"Moonrise," A. H. Alker	875
"September Noon," A. H. Alker	1,550
"A Silver Morning," W. H. Granberry	2,750
"Storm on the Delaware," W. H. Granberry	3,550
Total	$31,350

www.ingramcontent.com/pod-product-compliance
Lightning Source LLC
Chambersburg PA
CBHW022201020726
47496CB00008B/2825